Taken

By The

Highlander

A Historical Romance

Jessica Wolf

FREE BOOK!

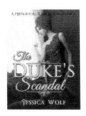

Get Your Free Copy of my never re-

leased book **The Duke's Scandal**

when you sign up for the authors VIP

mailing list here.

http://bit.ly/1OhfN5l

CONTENTS

I sigh as I run my brush through the last tangle of my wild mass of brown hair. Today's the day of the feast at the House of Stuart. Oh what I wouldn't give to spend my evening cozied by the fire writing a letter to mum back in the country side...

"Come on dear. You shan't be late for His Majesty," Elsa the young handmaiden chides me as she hands me my cream silk shawl.

I stand from the seat of my vanity and give myself a toaty once over before I leave. I felt grand. The bodice of my crème colored dress is adorned with pearls and the skirts give my arse a magnificent curve. It's too bad I have to spend the entirety of my evening in it. It looks wonderful but my breathing is difficult and my revealing cleavage makes me feel like a harlot at the local brothel.

I wrap my shawl tighter and head out of the door to my chambers and into the hallway, escorted by two of His Majesty's finest knights. I nod in acknowledgement and take slow, deliberate steps towards the dining room where His Majesty awaits me.

I smile at the thought for a moment of being the queen escorted by her knights. The thought is fleeting as I round the last turn to the dining room and catch a glimpse of the lady servant I saw heading into his chambers last night. She's batting her eyelashes at him as she sets down a plate of veal in front of a noble a few seats away from him. My smile turns into a dainty frown as I make my way to the seat at his right. I curtsey out of respect to His Majesty, and wait for a knight to pull my seat out for me.

I flash him my most savory grin that speaks a thousand unspoken words. In my opinion, the young lass needs to understand the difference between the people sitting at the table and the people serving the table.

"Aila, you look magnificent as always, dear," his smooth baritone voice resonates in my ears like the choir at mass. It's a beautiful symphony of power, wealth and beauty. It's a voice I could wake up to every morning.

"Thank you, Your Majesty. You look handsome as ever. Thank you once again for your hospitality," I reply.

The lady servant strides in and places a steaming dish of lamb in front of me and I take the moment to get a fine look at her. She really is quite pretty with blonde hair, piercing blue eyes, and a body that stands out even in peasant wear.

I pick up my fork and knife and daintily begin picking at my food.

Dinner passes by quickly and I'm glad once it's finally over. I've eaten just enough and have made some wonderful connections tonight. Mum and Dad will be happy about that. Everyone has left now and it's just me and His Majesty at the table.

"Aila, let's take a walk, shall we?"

"As you wish, Your Majesty." I felt my face blush and I tried to hide my face as I took his proffered hand to get out of my seat. I curtsey once more and I'm slightly surprised by his laughter that follows.

"Please, Aila, no need to be so formal when it's just you and I." I look up at him to see a grin that I rarely see on him. For once he looks like a carefree twenty-five year old lad. His smile was contagious and looking at him quickly warmed up my body. I return the favor with a smile as equally carefree.

"Yes, Your Majesty."

"Please, Aila, when we are in private please call me Clyde." He says.

For a brief moment, I wonder if the lady servant gets to call him Clyde but I push the thought out as quickly as it came in. I concede him with a smile as we make our way out of the dining room and to an exit that leads to the Royal Gardens. We stroll hand in hand and converse about nothing important. Soon enough, I started feeling weary from the horseback riding earlier on today.

He directs us to a bench and we take a seat, I lay my head lovingly on his broad chest.

"Aila, you can't fall asleep on me now, lass. I...I have something important to tell you." I stared up to look at his face. His gaze was different now. His eyes looked mysterious. His voice was tense and nervous. In all of our years of friendship and now courtship, he's never sounded nervous.

"Aila... Over the past ten years you and I have been such great friends and recently we've been courting..."

I felt my heart jump as excitement washed over me at my thoughts of where this is going... I've been waiting two years for this...

"I've had such a wonderful time and you're such a beautiful girl..."

I wonder what the ring looks like...

"It's so rare to be able to marry for love..."

Oh wait until I tell Mum...

"And even though it's rare, it's what I want..."

She's going to be so proud....

"So, I think we should end this."

For a moment, my mind stops working completely. For a moment, the garden fell silent and my heart stopped.

I turn, slowly, to him with my grin faltering just a little bit. I just looked at his eyes, not able to muster up words to speak. I should have known this would happen at some point. He's a king and I'm nobility but... I'm still from the House of Chalmers. As far as we've come, we're still not marriage material for a royal. I was foolish to even let the thought pervert my mind about marriage.

"As you wish, Your Majesty." I try to keep my grin even as I felt the tears welling up in my eyes. My jaw clenched as I tried to hold back the tears.

"Aila, I didn't mean to hurt you..." He looks genuinely sorry but he is a king. He's been trained to look genuine his entire life.

"I'm not hurt, Your Majesty." I fold my hands in my lap and continue to force a grin even as I started to feel the regret of everything I've worked so hard for during past two years of courtship slip away from me.

"Aila, please, I told you to call me Clyde."

"I'm not hurt, Clyde. I understand. May I take my leave now? I'd like to rest before I leave tomorrow morning." I stand up and brush my skirts off so I can have a reason to look away from him for a moment. When I look up at his face, all I see is pity.

v

"Aye, Aila. I won't be able to see you off in the morning but I wish you a safe trip."

I left the Royal Gardens that night with tears streaming down my face.

"ila!"

I groan and roll over in my bed, hoping the little wench will just leave and stop her horrid pounding on the doors of my chambers.
"Aila, wake up!"

If I were to be so lucky...

I have only a moment's respite from my sister's wretched yelling for me to awaken before I hear my lock rattling. I'm glad I locked it...

Only for her to pick the lock.

I gape at her for a moment as she bounds into my room, happy as a lark. At thirteen she can easily be mistaken for a lass of eighteen years. It's not always a good thing.

"Ainsley, what are you doing? You're not some pick pocketing peasant! How dare you!"

"Oh, Miss Aila, from the House of Chalmers, please oh please spare me the rod! I need my right hand! I have cello lessons at four!"

My little sister is an adorable character full of humor, light, and youth. It doesn't take me long to break down into a fit of giggles with her as she crawls into my bed.

"Aila, can you please get out of bed! The seamstress said my dress would be ready today and I need to try it on before the party," she gives me the most pitiful look she can muster. She looked like an adorable little puppy.

"Oh, I'm coming! Get out and let me get dressed. Have you seen Nilla anywhere?" I ask.

"She's making breakfast right now and she can't help you get dressed. Would you prefer Nissa?"

"No, Nissa is absolutely wretched. I'll do it by myself." I say.

She nods and smiles at me one last time and bounds back out of my room, leaving me to get ready for our day in town.

"Aila, don't I look lovely?" She twirls around in the emerald dress that hugs her body too closely for my liking but I must admit - she looks ravishing. The velvet bodice and soft silk skirts make her look closer to twenty than thirteen but she does it with class. Her blonde locks that refuse to be tamed fell by her waist and gave her a goddess-like look.

I nod in consent as the door opens and I turn to get a look at who's entering. I'm expecting another lass here for a fitting but instead what I see can be explained in three words; tall, Scottish, and handsome.

His face must have been hand sculpted by The Lord Our Father himself. His piercing green eyes stood out beneath a forest of rich, curly black hair, his cheekbones and strong jawline accentuated his plump lips that are beckoned me to kiss them, his broad shoulders led to a narrow waist carved by hard work on the farms, and his legs were elegant and strong. He was a symbol of perfection.

He flashes me a cheeky grin. I smile back and he bows out of respect. I acknowledge him with a nod and I shy away as I felt his gaze on me.

"Come on, Maddock please be respectful to lass and tell me what you came here for already," Leena chastises him as she escorts my sister into the separate changing room to take off the dress.

"I came to deliver the order of wool you needed. Andrew's in the back now, unloading the cart," he leans against the doorframe while he's talking, crossing his arms over his chest and the cheeky grin never leaves his face.

"Well then, shut your mouth and unload the cart, boy! Don't just stand there and make the lad do it all himself!" Leena calls out from behind the draw near the changing room.

Ainsley and the seamstress reappear together from the changing area and I notice something different about him. He doesn't leer at my little sister in the most unsavory way like most men do. He looks at her with a kind affection like someone should be showing to a lass of her age. I can tell instantly there's no malicious or sultry intent behind his gaze and it's something that brings a small smile to my face.

I watch him turn on his heel, and he's gone as quickly as he came.

"Aila, I know you weren't just eyeing that lad! I mean really... to go from being involved with a man of pure rebrov to looking at... that...that twally," said Ainsley as she handed over the coin to Leena for the dress. Leena gives me a knowing look but I can't help but think... the King swicked me a few times anyways. Why after being involved with him, no man will come near me out of fear of what he would do.

Unfortunately, Clyde has made no inferences that he could possibly care about me anymore. Three months have passed and I haven't received so much as a letter after my stay at the castle.

"Oh hush, Ainsley. I was simply being polite. Now, let's get on home so we can make it home before supper," I say.

CHAPTER TWO

S upper is quiet. Mum and Dad sit at the head of the table while Ainsley and I pick at our food. Our table is loud with the silence of my eldest brother Duff, who died at sea. Nobody makes a remark outside of telling Mum her food is delicious.

After supper, Mum is crocheting in the den while I braid Ainsley's freshly washed locks in an effort to keep her hair in some sort of semblance.

"So, Ainsley dear, how do you like your new dress?" Mum asks.

Her hands move with steady rhythm as she looks up from her work to speak to us. Nissa enters the room quietly with tea for all of us. Her and Mum exchange quick smiles before she exits the room again.

"Oh, Mum it's gorgeous! But that's not the only thing that happened at the seamstress today." I can hear the naughtiness in her voice and I pull her hair a little rougher than I need to in an effort to get her to keep her mouth shut.

"Oh is that so dear?" Mum's gaze flickers to me for a moment and her smile drops just a little bit before her gaze returns to Ainsley.

"Yes, Aila was giving a peasant eyes mum! I mean, he was handsome but seriously you should have seen the rags he was wearing." I yank her hair hard enough this time to make her yelp and start braiding faster. I don't let my eyes leave the back of her head but I can feel Mum's glare.

"Did she now?" Mum's tone is not one of question. It's a warning. It's a warning that I take heed to.

CHAPTER THREE

The coach rattles as we head down the path to the House of Ferguson. I stare out the window, not interested in the conversation going on between my sisters around me. I'm thankful that I'm not in the coach with Mum and Dad tonight but I would be most thankful if I was at home.

"Aila?" I look over to my eldest sister, Ailsa who has joined us for the evening.

"Yes?"

"Well, what do you think?" She raises an eyebrow in question at me and I can feel the heat rushing to my face.

"About what?" I ask.

"About that Ferguson lad. He would be great to court. His father is involved with the Royal Court. It would be smart of you, lass." She says.

"Aila is too busy thinking about peasant Scottish boys," Ainsley chimes in. Her melodic sing song voice does nothing except annoy me tonight. Ever since she mentioned him to Mum weeks ago, she's been bringing it up at every chance she possibly can and it's driving me absolutely mad. It's bad enough Mum is disappointed in me for losing Clyde, this has only added insult to injury.

"Ainsley, stop. You're acting like a huddy," I snap. I give her a glare to get my point across.

"Oh stop being such a fanny," she snaps back and returns my glare.

"If you two want to act like peasants and have such filthy mouths, why don't you go to the barn when we arrive? Really, you two should be ashamed! We're nobility, not pigs. Now, act like it." Ailsa's tone leaves no room for argument and Ainsley and I simmer down.

The rest of the ride is silent, and soon we're outside of the Ferguson estate. Our driver helps us out and I get a good look around. Every major family is here tonight. The Smiths, the Browns, the Scott family; everyone who is important is here.

I forget my argument with Ainsley instantly as I see my long time best friend Caroline getting out of her coach with her brother, John. I let Ainsley and Ailsa head inside while I wait at the top of the steps leading into the home for Caroline.

I search the crowd with my eyes for any of my other friends and get lost in trying to find them that I don't feel my fan slip out of my hand. It's not until a smooth tenor voice comes from behind me that I'm snap out of my thoughts.

"Would you like this back, Miss?" He asks from behind me.

As I turn, my jaw drops. Mason... or Michael... or whoever it was from the seamstress stands before me dressed like nobility and holding my fan.

After a few seconds, my senses return and I realize that Caroline didn't see me. It occurred to me that I've been standing here with my jaw dropped, staring at him. I snap it shut quickly, not wanting to be stricken and offer a polite smile. He doesn't look angry which is good but something looks different about him tonight besides his clothing.

"Thank you, sire... I remember you from the seamstress... what was your name again?" I smile and hope he doesn't get horribly offended by lack of remembrance. The last thing I need is to be stricken at such an important event because I can't remember a name.

"That's a little odd since I don't remember you. But, my name is Andrew. What's your name, lass?" He gives me another gentle smile and I reciprocate even though I'm completely lost. I could've sworn his name was Michael.

"My name is Aila, sire. My apologies. I could've sworn I saw you at the seamstress a few weeks ago..." I look at the ground hoping to alleviate some of the burning I feel in my cheeks and pray someone interrupts us. Luckily, I get my wish.

"Andrew dear," comes a pleasant woman's voice behind us.

"Isabelle, love, you look amazing." I turn around and get a look at her. I recognize her from a few events and make a mental note to become acquainted with her sometime this evening.

"Thank you. I didn't know you knew Miss Chalmers," her brow furrows in confusion at us and I try and clear the situation up but Andrew beats me to it.

"I don't. She dropped her fan. I was simply being a gentleman. Now, would you like to head inside?"

"Yes, of course. Thank you, sire." This time, my brow furrows as she transitions from addressing him with such familiarity to acting like she hardly knows him.

I watch them head inside and decide after a moment that I should follow.

The night ends quickly. I see no sign of Andrew again for the rest of the night and I'm having trouble keeping my balance with all of the wine I drank. I managed to make acquaintances with the Isabelle lass and found Caroline after some time and even had a few almost pleasant drinks with my mum. The night went pretty well.

It's not until I'm back in the coach with Ainsley and Ailsa that I think about Andrew again. My thoughts are hazy from inebriation and I can't help but think about the fact that I could've sworn his name was Michael.

"I know you saw him, Aila," Ainsley says. She doesn't look up from her seat across from me.

"Of course you do." I reply. I don't bother with snapping or even looking at her. I'm tired, inebriated, and confused.

CHAPTER FOUR

T he next morning, I felt like an absolute wreck. I'm tired and I have the worst hangover that I've had in a while. I simply lie in bed until I hear a knock at my door.

"Madame, your father would like for you to come downstairs," Nilla calls to me.

"Okay, Nill, I'm coming." I reply.

I get out of bed and throw on a simple white dress and make my way downstairs.

When I get to the kitchen, I see Dad sipping his morning tea dressed in riding breeches. I hope we'll be spending some time together today...

"Aye, mornin' lass. Did ye sleep well?" He asks. He gives me a lopsided grin that I return pleasantly.

"Yes, Dad. I did. How about yourself?" I reply.

"Of course. Now, I was thinking we could go riding this morning. I have to go to a farm not too far from here and look at some animals. Care to join honey?"

"Yes, that sounds lovely, Daddy." I reply.

CHAPTER FIVE

The farm is... quaint. Daddy and I arrive on our horses around noon and I take a moment to look around. There's a ramshackle pig sty, a simple lean-to for the horses, a few cows, and the chickens roamed freely. The house is... cute. It's smaller than mine but looks relatively well-made.

Daddy and I tie our horses to the post out in front of the house and walk up the steps to the front door. He knocks a few times and we wait.

Less than a minute later, a young lass probably Ainsley's age, opens the door for us.

"Aye, welcome Mister and Miss Chalmers. Can I help ye?" I smile politely at her and think about how some elocution lessons would really do her wonders. They certainly helped me.

"Aye, Miss Buchanon. Is Andrew or Maddock around?" Daddy says. I feel my eyes widen just the slightest bit at the realization that this is the lad's house from last night as well as a few weeks ago from the seamstress...

"Aye, I'm right here, sire." We both turn around to get a look at the owner of the voice and I see it's the lad from last night. He's dressed accordingly today in what looks to be hand-me-down breeches and a simple cotton shirt. It's nothing elaborate.

"Andrew, me lad! How're ye doin?" Daddy asks with a smile.

"I'm doing well, sire. And how about yerself? Maddock's got them bessies up in the shed fer ye to get a look at if you will. And I-" he stops suddenly as he gets a look at me for the first time. His eyes widen fractionally but nobody except me notices. "Aye, mornin' miss. Chassy, get the lass some tea, please. Stop just standin' there with yer geggy open, lass!"

I turn away from him and Daddy and follow Chassy into the house. When I walk in, I'm surprised. It's furnished nicely and the family portraits show the three siblings and their parents. The one thing I notice is that while Andrew and Maddock look like their father, Chassy looks like their mom with her blue eyes and blonde hair.

"Aye, miss would ye like a seat?" She asks while she gets to work setting up a tea pot.

"Yes, thank you." I smile politely and wait for her to fix tea. I take a look at my surroundings. The kitchen is simple with wooden walls that match the exterior of the house, a few paintings hang here and there, a door that leads outside, a table that fits five for eating, and an odd little pillow in the corner.

"So, where do you go to school, Chassy?" I ask.

"I go to school down yonder in town. I believe your mum is a teacher there? Misses Beattie right?" She asks.

"Yes, she is lass. Do you like school there?"

"Aye, I do Madame. It's nice to get away from the farm a few times a week." She says.

She finishes with my tea and pours me a cup, setting it down in front of me. I smile in thanks and add some cream and sugar from the lazy Susan in front of me. As I take my first sip, the door in the kitchen opens. Someone rushes in and starts... panting?

I set my tea down in time to see a little hound of some type, it must be a mutt since I can't identify it. It ran over to the odd little pillow and laid down. It's absolutely filthy. It's caked in mud, probably dung of some sort and seemed to be full of fleas. I can't for the life of me fathom why on earth it's allowed in the house.

"Aye, Chassy, can you fix me a cup of tea? Me head is loopin' from last night." The man says. I recognize his voice instantly from the seamstress but I can't for the life of me turn my head around to say hello. I just pray that I look nice today even after riding horses in this horrid weather. I didn't see him at the party last night so I wonder why he's hungover...

"Mornin' lass." He says. He takes a moment to pull out a chair across from me. When he sits down, his face is shocked with an expression of surprise and then pleasure. He gives me the same gentle smile he did a few weeks ago and I can't help the meek smile that crosses my face. Aye, I am officially in trouble.

"Morning, sire. How are you today?" I ask.

"I'm doing well, Madame." He says. He sips his tea and his piercing eyes never leave mine. Chassy leaves without saying a word and I feel rather uncomfortable.

"So, um... I saw your brother last night. Where were you?" I ask.

He flashes me a wolf like grin and I can't help but wonder if he was with his girlfriend or something...

"I was at me bird's house, lass." He says. I knew it. Nobody, rich or poor and that good looking is single.

"Oh. And who would that be?" I ask.

"None of ye business, lass." He says. I'm offended but I don't pry. I just look down at my tea, awkwardly, and play with my hands. "Aye, lass I'm kidding. Take a joke, will ye?"

I look up, searching his face for the truth. The look on his face is playful and I can't help but start giggling myself.

"Sire, you threw me for a loop there. I thought you were serious." I say as I giggled harder.

"Maybe if I was talking about ye, I would be." He says confidently. I look up at him, my jaw dropped slightly and decide now is the perfect time for a sip of my tea.

"Lad, you don't know me." I say as I adjusted my posture.

"I'd like to. How about ye meet me again tonight at the tavern. We get some drinks and get to know one another." He says. He smiles at me and I'm expecting him to look somewhat desperate like most men but as I looked up, I felt an unwavering demeanor in his green eyes.

"Which tavern?" I ask.

"Bettson's. Right down yonder," he says.

"Bettson's... I've never been there before. What's the dress code?" I ask.

"Dress like a peasant, lass." He says with a wink.

"Maybe..." I say.

"I'll be there whether you come or not, lassie." He says.

Suddenly, the door opens again to reveal Andrew and my father traipsing in, covered in mud.

"Yes, lad, I'll have someone come by tomorrow and get them sallies and a few bessies. I'll have to talk to me wife about that stud colt ye got but he seems like a good horse." My dad says.

"Aye, sire, he's bred sturdy and would make a great work or riding horse."

"Well, lad, me and the lady must be getting' on. It was good workin' with ye. We'll be seeing ye folks around." My dad says.

With that, we head out and make our way back home. I ponder about going to the tavern tonight...

CHAPTER SIX

I look at myself in the mirror. I look... like a peasant. Nissa was kind enough to not only lend me a dress, but lend me a dress with no questions or talking to my parents about it. My hair is in a simple braid and the dress isn't the usual silk or svelte I'm used to. It's a scratchy cotton material that bunches in the most unflattering places.

I sigh and tie a simple brown cloak around my shoulders, preparing for the evening to come. I have to remind myself that I won't get caught , that Mum and Dad went to bed an hour ago and are probably fast asleep by now. I repeat the words 'I won't get caught' like I'm praying to the Lord Our Father himself. Heaven knows I'll need his help pulling this off....

I quietly make my way down the stairs and out of the back door without being seen. I'm thankful that the night sky is clear tonight and there's no rain. The moon and stars shine clearly tonight and finding my mare's tack is easy. I'm saddled in under five minutes and trotting down the road towards town.

My mind reels in circles about potential problems and the fear of being recognized. I don't know many peasants but I come from a prominent family, they might know me. Even worse, they might know my Mum and Dad... I push the negative thoughts to the back of my mind as I see the lanterns lighting up the buildings in town as I ride down the path.

Everywhere looks closed down for the night except for a rickety building on my left so I assume it's the place I'm supposed to be heading and I guide my mare that way. As I get closer, I see a few gentlemen drunkenly smoking on the porch of the building and hear Scottish music coming from inside. Yes, this is definitely the place I'm supposed to be heading.

I tie my mare to the post in front with the other horses and pull down the hood of my cloak. My heart was racing as I walk up the steps. I hear a few whistles and cat calls from the gentlemen on the porch and ignore them. When I open the door, I'm hit with the smell of alcohol, smoke, and lots of sweaty people. Everyone is dancing to the small band of merry players on a not so sturdy looking stage and with all of these people, I can't find Maddock anywhere.

I ignore the men and women alike who stare at me and search the crowd, slowly heading towards the bar. Everywhere that I looked I saw no familiar faces. I sigh and take a seat at the bar. I ignore the leering looks of the gentlemen who look old enough to be my grandfather and turn around to face the crowd.

"Aha! You showed up." I turn to look at the voice that seemed to come out of nowhere from behind me. Across the bar, washing a cup with a rag, is Maddock.

"Um, I wasn't aware you worked here." I say. I hope my voice doesn't sound too disappointed but now I understand what he meant earlier about showing up either way. Part of me is slightly relieved that he's not here out of choice.

"Aye, sweetie. The cost of livin' is goin' up. Andrew, Chassy, and me are considerin' movin' back to Scotland soon. We don't belong in these parts, we were born high-landers" He says.

"I wonder what it's like over there sometimes." I reply. He offers me a kind smile as he turns his back to put the cup back in its rightful place. Before he comes back to me, he refills a shot of whiskey for a gentlemen to my right and fills a pint of ale for someone. I expect him to hand the pint to another gentlemen but instead he sets it down in front of me and goes back to getting another pint.

He returns with another pint a moment later for himself and takes a long swig. I don't move. I've only ever drank champagne, wine, or liquor and even that's rare for me.

"C'mon, lassie, it's ale not poison." He says with a grin. He leans against the bar and sends me a charming grin. I take the pint by both hands, took a gulp and shut my eyes hard at the foul taste. "That's it, sweetie."

"You know, I came here because I thought you were going to be on the other side of the bar..." I say while taking another sip that is considerably smaller than the gulp I decided to take.

Without warning he sits on the bar then throws his legs over, effectively ending up on the other side of the bar. He slips gracefully onto the seat next to me and slides his pint of ale over as well.

"Better, Lass?" He says. I smile in answer and take another sip.

"Maddock! Come on! Dance!" Shouts a feminine voice from behind us. He turns around in his seat and nods. He gets up and offers me his hand.

"Maddock I've never danced to... um..."

"This kind of music." He finishes the sentence for me and I can feel my face go red with embarrassment. "It's fun, lass. Just follow my lead and eventually you'll get into it."

"Okay..." I say. I follow him into the crowd and we get a spot close to the musicians. It's a lively beat with a lot of drum and banjo and I'm instantly caught up in trying to follow Maddock's smooth movements.

Once I finally feel confident in my movements and the fact that I won't be crushing his toes, I look up at him. He's grinning playfully down at me and spins me out. When he spins me back in, he dips me so low I think he's going to drop me. But, he doesn't drop me. Instead, he comes down low with me and for a moment I swear he's going to plant a chaste one on my lips but he doesn't. He comes so close that I can smell the alcohol on his breath and his natural scent that is a mix of pine and musk. I decide in that moment, it's my new favorite scent.

It takes me a moment to comprehend that for the first time in a long time, I'm having fun. Genuine, unbridled fun. I smiled back at him as we dance and two songs later, a familiar face shows up. Well, two familiar faces if you count my brief encounter with Isabelle last night. They dance in time with us and halfway through the song, Maddock and Andrew let go of both of us.

I don't understand what everyone expects of us for a moment but when Isabelle grabs me by my waist and sends me back into the same dancing routine I was enjoying with Maddock, it becomes crystal clear.

"Lass, I recognize ye!" She shouts over the din of the music and the crowd.

"Yes, lass! How have you been!" I shout back.

"Great! I'm surprised to see ye here! You should come out more often!"

"Hopefully, I will!" I give one last shout and we continue dancing.

When Isabelle spins me out, I get a look at Maddock who is standing next to Andrew and he's got a boyish grin on his face that clearly says 'I know something that you don't.' I don't have a moment to ponder it as Isabelle spins me back in and plants a big one right on my lips. My eyes widen in surprise and dare I say it-pleasure. The crowd goes absolutely wild as we delight in this forbidden act publicly and it's over all too soon. A moment later, Isabelle has parted from my lips looking flushed and we're both in a fit of giggles.

We're still laughing when I feel a strong arm around my waist and hear a deep voice in my ear.

"C'mon, lass, let's go get us another drink. I can't be losin' ye to Isabelle over here. I haven't even got me turn yet." He says. I can hear the smile in his voice and a tiny part of me is happy he's jealous of Isabelle.

"Okay, sire." I giggle.

"**A**nd that's how Andrew ended up chasing the pigs down the middle of town!" Maddock half shouts over the still lively crowd. We're on our fifth pint each and my world is spinning. I've never drank this much in my entire life.

"Aye, he sounds like a lad who can't shut his geggy long enough to do his dern job!" I shout back. My words are slurring and every elocution lesson I've ever taken can't save me right now.

"Lass, I'm gonna go outside for a smoke. Ye comin'?" He asks.

"I don't smoke but I'll come." I say. I slide off the stool and when I stand, I realize how drunk I really am. I sway a little bit but a stern arm steadies me and we walk out to the porch. Once we get outside, I see my faithful mare still at the post and lean against the railing of the porch.

Maddock lights up a rolled tobacco cigarette and lights it with a match. He steps over and leans on the railing beside me and we sit in companionable silence for a few moments. It gives me time to try and think over tonight. I haven't felt this alive and this free since my early days going around causing mischief with Duff.

"What're ye thinkin' bout, lass?" He asks me. I turn to face him and the only thing I can focus on are his lips.

"Just that I haven't have this much fun in a while." I reply. My gaze still doesn't leave his lips. They look so soft...

"Well, lass, ye should come with me more often. I bet we'd have loads more fun than this." He says. He puts out his cigarette even though there's more than half left and cups his hand around my face. I sigh and lean into his touch. His hands are calloused with years of hard work but they feel like hands that could protect me.

A moment later and I feel a pair of moist, warm lips on mine. His kiss starts out gentle at first but eventually, the desire grows and he gets more passionate. His hands travel to my waist and my hands tangle in his mass of curly black hair and we only separate when someone clears their throat from behind him.

Another gentlemen who has showed up to smoke a cigarette of his own gives us a disapproving look and then goes back to lighting up his cigarette.

Maddock smiles at me and takes my hand.

"Lass, it's awful late. Why don't you head home?" He says.

"Okay..." I reply. I walk down the steps, not letting go of his hand and untie my mare. Once I throw the reins over her neck, I come to the realization I have to let go of his hand and head home for the night.

I turn around to face him and I take a moment to realize that he stands a full head above me. He looks down at me with a kind close lipped smile and I return the favor. He leans down and plants a gentle kiss on my lips.

"I'm glad you're letting me get to know you, Aila. Come by the farm tomorrow, I don't have much work to do and I'd like to spend more time with you." He whispers in my ear. He wraps me in his arms and gives me a final hug and I rest my head on his chest for just a moment.

The moment ends too soon and soon I'm on my horse and heading away from the tavern. As I ride home, I think. I think about how six months ago, I was sneaking bottles of wine to the barn with Duff talking about the latest news between Clyde and I. I was concerned with which noble was wearing what and becoming the next queen. Tonight, I was concerned with having fun and doing things that were so naughty but felt so free.

I let a tear slide down my cheek at the fact that I can't tell my eldest brother about tonight's adventures-or any future adventures ever again. Of course I want to adventure to Scotland, but after losing Duff to the seas...

I don't let myself get too far into thought about him since I'm inebriated and now I'm coming up the road to my home and... a lantern is on?

My heart begins to race as I realize the implication of this small fact. Someone is waiting up for me. I'm crocked and in a peasant's dress. I was just out partying, reeking of alcohol and kissing girls at a tavern. I ride my horse to the barn and unsaddle as quickly as I possibly can. I try my best to walk in a straight line to the house.

As I walk in the kitchen, my worst fear is confirmed. My Mum is sitting at the table, with a bottle of whiskey open and staring at the door I just entered through. She stays silent and I take my chances and simply walk past her. She doesn't say anything to me as I continue on my way like absolutely nothing is wrong and head into my bedroom.

I take the cloak off, followed by what I've officially deemed as the most hideous dress in the world and slide under the covers of my bed in simply my undergarments. I'm too crocked to put anything else on. I fall asleep thinking about his green eyes and the Scotland highlands.

CHAPTER EIGHT

"Aila, do you know a lass named Isabelle?" My dad asks me. My thoughts rush immediately down the worst path possible that he knows about my tryst last night and kissing her but he continues reading the paper like it's nothing so I try to calm my nervous mind down. I walk to the stove and fix myself a cup of tea and then I sit down at the table with them.

"Yes, I saw her at a party recently. Why?" I ask. I take a sip of my tea and try to act like I don't feel my mother's gaze burning holes into me.

"Well, rumors have been going around that she's been involved with one of those Buchanon boys and your mum and I were just thinking how you should make sure to steer clear of her." He says.

"Yes, father." I say. I sip my tea some more as father gets up and puts on his overcoat. "Where are you going?" I ask.

"To the Buchanon farm. Gotta get them animals. Would you like to come with me?" He asks. I nod my head and try not to seem too eager.

We trot our horses down the small path leading to the Buchanon farm. The clip-clop of the horse's hooves match the rapid beating of my heart. I try not to smile too much as we approach and I see Andrew and Maddock unloading a few bags of feed from a cart. Andrew notices us first and motions for Maddock to stop working.

"Boys, what're ye up to today?" My dad asks.

"Just getting' rid of the last of the animals," Maddock says. I furrow my brow in confusion. Why would he be getting rid of the animals?

"Why?" I ask.

"We're headin' to Scotland. Back to the good ol' highlands," Andrew replies. I glance over at Maddock who has an unreadable expression on his face.

"Aye, laddies. Well, good luck to you. My boys are gonna round them animals back up to our house." My father replies.

Andrew motions for my father to follow him over to where the cows are and I'm left alone with Maddock.

"When are you fellows leaving?" I ask. I try to sound like I'm not disappointed.

"In a month." He replies.

"Why are you going?" I ask. Why can't he just stay?

"You know the answer, lass. It's no good over here for us. We need to head to where we belong, the highlands." He says.

"Oh... ok." I reply.

"Meet me at the tavern tonight. I...want to spend more time with you."

"Okay. I'll see you later then." I reply. I don't know why I agree, I'm just setting myself up for heartbreak ultimately but I want to see him again. I want to have that kind of fun again.

Andrew and my father appear from behind the ramshackle barn chatting away about something a few minutes later, and I see my dad give Andrew a companionable pat on the back.

"Aila, are ye ready to go?" My dad asks me.

"Yes, father. I am." I reply. We mount our horses and say our goodbyes.

CHAPTER NINE

The rain drizzles steadily on my cloak. I can see the lanterns of the town ahead and my heart starts to race with excitement for another fun night. I smile to myself at the thought of another night filled with dancing, drinking and having fun.

As I approach I notice Maddock is standing out front next to his horse. I continue on my way up to him.

"Aila, good to see you. I was hoping we could go somewhere else tonight." He says as he mounts his horse.

"Sure," I reply. He guides his horse down the path and we continue to leave town.

We spend our ride making idle conversation about nothing and everything. He tells me about his and Andrew's plans to start a farm in America and how Isabelle plans on leaving with them. I tell him about how I would love to see it one day. We talk for what seems like forever until we finally approach a wooded section of forest just outside the town.

We traipse through the woods on our horses for a few minutes until we come to a small clearing. At the edge of the clearing is a small pond. I furrow my brow in confusion as we dismount. Maddock takes a few items out of his saddle bags and I tie our horses to a nearby tree.

As I watch Maddock set up a blanket, a bottle of what looks to be champagne and some cards, I admire him. He looks calm, collected, and genuinely happy to be spending some time alone with me. I sit down on the blanket he set up for us and untie my cloak. He sits down across from me and uncorks the bottle, taking a large swig then offering it to me.

"So, Aila, you haven't really told me much about yourself yet." He says after I finish my first swig. "I believe I said I wanted to get to know you."

"Well, there isn't much to know. My family hails from our town, my father works in the banks when he's not working around the farm, I have two sisters and a brother..." I trail off at the mention of Duff without realizing it and I take another swig of the champagne. It tastes too strong.

"Was your brother Duff Chalmers?" He asks, taking the bottle from me and taking a swig of his own.

"Yes, he was. We were very close." I reply. A wave of sadness hits me as I think about him. I've tried for so long to avoid thinking about him. "Why do you ask?"

"Just curious is all, lass." He takes another swig and passes the bottle back to me. As I take another swig, I start to feel the effects of the alcohol finally setting in. "So, what do ye want to do?"

"What do you mean?" I ask.

"I mean... with your life. Do ye wanna get married and stay here in England, do ye wanna move to Scotland to the Highlands. What do ye wanna do?" I smile at his Scottish country accent and take another swig.

"Honestly, I want to leave. I want to go somewhere free. Somewhere I'm not judged for who I want to be with or who I want to be. Somewhere I can raise a lot of kids who are free." I say. I've never admitted it before. Not even to myself.

"So then leave." He says. His gaze holds mine steady and we each take another swig.

CHAPTER TEN

The weeks pass and Maddock and I continue to meet every night and talk about nothing and everything. We grow closer and closer and as we see each other less and less around town, we make up for it in the time we spend together at night alone. He becomes my best friend outside of my sisters and I feel happy for the first time in months. He encourages me to be myself.

"I think you should come with us," Isabelle says. We're sitting in the tavern in our peasant disguises drinking our third pint while the boys sit a few tables away betting on an arm wrestling match between two men.

I take another chug of my ale and reply. "You know what, I just might. I'm tired of this place anyways. It's boring. There's nothing to do here. I want be free."

"Then come with us! We leave in a week from now. It'll be amazing. You, me, Andy, Chassy, and Maddock. We can all get a huge piece of land and start a farm. Just picture it; green grass, cows, children playing in a few years." She says. She crosses her legs and props her chin on her hand as she thinks. Her offer really is quite enticing. I take another swig and think that she could be onto something.

I'm snapped out of my thoughts as a pair of strong arms wrap around my waist from behind and someone presses a warm pair of lips to my neck.

"Aila, it's late. You should be getting' on home." He says into my ear. I lean back into his broad chest and place my hands over his at my waist.

"Yes, I should." I say. I get up and say goodbye to Isabelle and we make our way out to the horses. As I'm about to mount, I turn to say goodbye to Maddock.

"I want to leave," I say. He looks surprised for a moment and then his surprise turns into elation.

"So then leave." He says. He wraps his arms around my waist and pulls me close to him, enveloping me in his warmth.

"I want to leave with you." He presses his forehead to mine so are lips are inches apart.

"So then leave with me." He replies. I inhale his natural pine musk scent mixed with whiskey and smile.

"Seven days." I say.

"Seven days."

CHAPTER ELEVEN

I finish the bird design that I've been crocheting for a few hours now and put down my tools. I look over to Ainsley who is reading a book and at Ailsa, who has decided to visit again. I contemplate telling them of my plans to leave for Scotland and take a few deep breaths. If I can trust anyone, it's them.

"Do you ever want to leave?" I ask. They both look up at me simultaneously. Ainsley has a look of understanding on her face while Ailsa looks like she could strike me down at this very moment.

"Why would we want to?" She snaps.

"For freedom." I reply calmly. I sip my tea and hold her fierce gaze.

"You have freedom." She says. Her voice is quiet in warning but I throw caution to the wind.

"It sounds like fun." Ainsley says. Her voice is quiet and her face is somber.

"I'm sure Duff would disagree," Ailsa snaps. Ainsley's resolve weakens and she goes back to reading quietly.

I say nothing after that. The rejection from her and my mother is only strengthening my resolve to leave and never look back. Even if I made it to England and never looked back, I would be happy. So long as I wasn't here.

The evening passes by quickly. I pack a few of my things in small knapsack and I planned my escape. My plan is to slowly move things so Maddock can have them when we leave so nobody get's too suspicious. I put in a simple dress, some jewelry and some money and tie the bag shut.

I pull my cloak on and make my way to the barn to mount my mare. Soon, we're on our way to the Buchanon farm.

As I arrive, I see Maddock sitting on the porch with Chassy in an animated conversation. Maddock's face is alight with mirth and Chassy looks like she's ready to strike him at any moment. I dismount and they turn their attention to me.

"Aila! Hello, lassie!" Chassy greets me. She's jubilant as she bounds over to give me a hug. "Here, give me your things and I'll go add them to the trunk I'm taking."

She takes my knapsack and heads inside, leaving me alone with Maddock.

"I'm glad she likes you. She's been lonesome since Mum passed away." He says.

"Yes, me too. How long has it been by the way?" I ask. I realize I've never asked about their parents, just like he doesn't ask about Duff.

"It's been about four years. Mum and Dad both got sick within weeks of each other. Andrew and I were gone doing some business for the farm but Chassy was here with the nursemaid who also got sick. She was old and couldn't handle the sickness, passed a few weeks right after Mum and Dad." He says. He walks up to me and wraps his arms around my waist, pulling me close. "Are you ready, love? Only a few more days and we'll be gone."

"More than ready." I reply with a smile on my face. As he looks at me, his smile fades. I furrow my brows in question until he gets down on one knee.

"Aila, I know that we haven't known each other long but... the past few months have been incredible. I know you're a good woman and I want you to be mine and nobody else's. I can't tell you in words how deeply I've grown to care for you over the past few months. You're someone I want to spend the rest of my days with. Please... when we get to Scotland and we're settled down, marry me." He looks up at me with hope and nervousness in his eyes and I can't help but smile. He takes a small diamond ring out of his pocket and places it on my left ring finger.

"Where did you get this?" I ask, astonished.

"It was my Mum's. Take good care of it." He replies. He stands back up and gives me a long kiss.

The rest of the night is incredibly relaxing. Maddock and I sit by the fire recollecting stories of our youth and telling jokes while Chassy crochets and occasionally adds an anecdote or two of her much to Maddock's chagrin. I realize that I love the story of Maddock falling off of a horse he swore he could train at twelve years old and crying in his room for an hour. I realize I love sitting with him and his family talking about nothing and everything. There's no uncomfortable silence or limits on the conversation. We talk about being free in the highlands, what animals we want to have, what we want and when silence does fall, it's companionable. Unlike home, the silence isn't awkward because someone said the wrong thing or because someone can't move past losing someone. I realize I'm surrounded by people who have lost people and they're just fine. These are the people I want to spend my life with.

Five days later, I'm with Maddock, Andrew, Chassy, Isabelle, and even Maddock's dog loading onto the cart in the middle of the night. We pack our things on as tightly as we can and steer the horses pulling the cart to the docks where we'll board a ship and sail to Scotland.

Goodbye England, you have my heart no longer. I am running away with a Highlander.

THE END

Recommended Book On Highlander Romance

I hope you have enjoyed my Highlander book! If you're interested in learning more about Highlander Romance, check out this book which I highly recommend.

Healing a Highlander's Heart by Keira Montclair

Check it out here: http://amzn.to/1ejuJTA

Happy reading! ☺

From the Author

Thank you for purchasing my book. Your loving support allows me to continue doing a job I love every day. If you liked this story, please consider leaving a review so more people can find and enjoy my books.

Hugs,

Jessica Wolf :)

P.S. – If you have any questions about this book, please email me at authorjessicawolf@gmail.com first and I will ensure that any issues get addressed. I read every email from you guys and I would love to hear about what you guys think!

Kindle Unlimited subscribers
read this entire catalog for FREE!

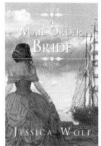

Mail Order Bride Romance

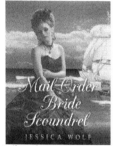

Mail Order Bride Romance

Highlander Romance

Mail Order Bride Romance

Regency Historical Romance

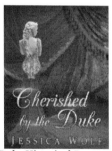

Duke Historical Romance

FREE BOOK!

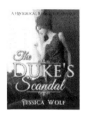

Get Your Free Copy of my never released

book **The Duke's Scandal** when you sign

up for the authors VIP mailing list here.

http://bit.ly/1OhfN5l

ABOUT THE AUTHOR

Jessica Wolf's Page: http://amzn.to/1J9IHUa

Jessica Wolf was raised in Texas, but after graduating from high school, she moved to Ohio to become a registered nurse, spending most of her career bringing a smile to her patients. She became a freelance fiction writer and president of her local writing chapter. Writing is something she has always loved and plans on doing for a long time into the future.

Jessica Wolf is a mother, a writer, and a wife. Married to the love of her life for seventeen years, she knows that real love exists in this world and wants to share her vision with her readers. She writes historical romance as well as inspirational. She invites you to venture into her world of fantasy to experience lost love, true love and hope.

Printed in Poland
by Amazon Fulfillment
Poland Sp. z o.o., Wrocław

53887697R00040